1-2-3

A Calmer Me

for Dennis, who keeps me calm and balanced — *CAP*
for Donnell, who is kind, calm and caring — *BSM*

for Sean and Micky, with all my love — *CK*

Published by
M A G I N A T I O N   P R E S S®
An Educational Publishing Foundation Book
American Psychological Association
750 First Street, NE
Washington, DC 20002

Magination Press is a registered trademark of the American Psychological Association.

For more information about our books, including a complete catalog, please write to us, call 1-800-374-2721, or visit our website at www.apa.org/pubs/magination.

Book design by Susan K. White
Printed by Phoenix Color Corporation, Hagerstown, MD

Library of Congress Cataloging-in-Publication Data
Patterson, Colleen A., author.
1-2-3 a calmer me : helping children cope when emotions get out of control /
by Colleen A. Patterson, MA, and Brenda S. Miles, PhD ; illustrated by Claire Keay.
pages cm
Summary: A young girl learns a technique for dealing with anger—and it works.
ISBN 978-1-4338-1931-5 (hardcover) — ISBN 1-4338-1931-7 (hardcover) —
ISBN 978-1-4338-1932-2 (pbk.) — ISBN 1-4338-1932-5 (pbk.) 1. Anger—Juvenile fiction.
2. Calmness—Juvenile fiction. 3. Emotions—Juvenile fiction. [1. Anger—Fiction.
2. Calmness—Fiction. 3. Emotions—Fiction.] I. Miles, Brenda, author. II. Keay, Claire,
illustrator. III. Title. IV. Title: One two three a calmer me.
PZ7.1.P38Aah 2015
[E]—dc23
                                                    2014031515

Manufactured in the United States of America
First printing April 2015
10 9 8 7 6 5 4 3 2 1

JJ
PATTERSON
COLLEEN

1-2-3

A Calmer Me

**Helping Children Cope
When Emotions
Get Out of Control**

by Colleen A. Patterson, MA and Brenda S. Miles, PhD
illustrated by Claire Keay

MAGINATION PRESS • WASHINGTON, DC
American Psychological Association

I am happy, but sometimes I feel mad and VERY frustrated!

Like the other day when I let go of my balloon.

I felt s-o-o-o mad!

My friend told me it's okay to feel mad,
but there's something I can do to feel better.

I can stop and say a rhyme that has some actions.

Let's try the rhyme together!

1-2-3 a calmer me

1-2-3 I hug me

Give yourself a BIG hug, nice and tight!

1-2-3 relax and b-r-e-a-t-h-e

Take a BIG breath in and let it out s-l-o-w-l-y…

1-2-3 a calmer me

Pretend your arms are jelly and let your hug s-l-i-d-e away.

I'm glad my friend showed me
what to do! When I stopped
and said the rhyme it slowed
my body down and helped me
get rid of my mad feelings.

The next day when I had to
stop playing, I felt mad again!

I tried saying the rhyme by myself.

1-2-3 a calmer me

1-2-3 I hug me

1-2-3 relax and b-r-e-a-t-h-e

1-2-3 a calmer me

Guess what?
It worked!
The mad feelings
got smaller and
I felt better!

Now I say the rhyme whenever I need it and wherever I go. I say it when someone takes my favorite red crayon.

1-2-3 a calmer me

1-2-3 I hug me

1-2-3 relax and b-r-e-a-t-h-e

1-2-3 a calmer me

Then I feel calm and ready
to play with my friends!

When schoolwork is hard, I say the rhyme again.

1-2-3 a calmer me

1-2-3 I hug me

1-2-3 relax and b-r-e-a-t-h-e

1-2-3 a calmer me

It works!
I feel calm and
try my best!

When I play sports, I say the rhyme
because no one wins all the time!

1-2-3 a calmer me

1-2-3 I hug me

1-2-3 relax and b-r-e-a-t-h-e

1-2-3 a calmer me

Some days
I still get mad
and frustrated.

But when I say my rhyme
I feel s-o-o-o much better!

Note to Parents, Teachers, and Other Grown-Ups

At one time or another, you have probably witnessed a child's emotions spinning out of control. When children are upset, it can be frustrating for parents, teachers, and any grown-up. Without your help, children may resort to hitting, kicking, biting, screaming, or crying when they feel frustrated, challenged, or disappointed. When children behave this way, we often tell them to stop. While these behaviors need to change, remember that upset or uncomfortable feelings are okay. Part of growing up is learning how to handle those feelings in ways that make us feel better. In this book, the rhyme "1-2-3 A Calmer Me" is a simple mantra for helping children cope when their emotions start spinning out of control.

Emotions Start in the Brain

Everyone experiences uncomfortable emotions—both adults and children—and we all react to them. Emotions start in the brain, in a collection of structures called the limbic system. The limbic system reacts to situations that are scary, new, and annoying. Sometimes our reactions happen so fast that we act before we think. But when we think first, we can slow down our reactions and maybe even change them. Thinking first means we activate the part of our brain behind the forehead called the frontal lobes. The frontal lobes help put the brakes on our immediate reactions and give us time to consider a more effective, and less impulsive, response. So why do young children seem to react so quickly with big emotions when they are upset? Well, children's frontal lobes are not fully developed. In fact, the frontal lobes are still developing in early adulthood! Since children's frontal lobes are still developing, young children tend to react impulsively to uncomfortable emotions and upset feelings. It's important, then, to slow down children's immediate reactions and replace them with responses that are more comforting. The mantra "1-2-3 A Calmer Me" can be used with children already able to handle their emotions well and with those who are struggling.

Pre-Teaching the Basics

The "1-2-3 A Calmer Me" mantra can be used with children anywhere, anytime. The approach is based on the psychological principles of *relaxation* (allowing your body to release stress) and *mindfulness* (being aware of what is around you and taking time to think before you act). The mantra encourages *deep breathing* (taking slow and relaxed breaths) and *progressive muscle relaxation* (a process of tensing and then relaxing muscles). The repetitive rhyme is easy to learn, even for preschoolers. But first, children need to practice.

Teach the steps when your child is calm and able to focus so the mantra and actions can be called upon more easily in times of distress.

"1-2-3 a calmer me": Some children may not understand the word "calm." Explain that being "calm" means feeling relaxed, like when you are listening to a bedtime story or cuddling a stuffed toy. A "calmer me" means changing your upset or frustrated feelings into feelings that are relaxed.

"1-2-3 I hug me": Hugging is the first action in the mantra. Teach your child to give him- or herself a big, tight hug. In times of distress, this action should help to contain hands and lessen the urge to pinch, slap, punch, or scratch. Encourage your child to lock—or squeeze—his or her body with that hug; a locked body is still and wrapped in a tight hug with feet glued to the ground. Glued feet stay put and do not run or kick. When the body is locked, it is tight, allowing the process of progressive muscle relaxation to begin. By the end of the mantra, your child should recognize the difference between a tense body and a relaxed one. For older children who may wish to be more discreet during self-calming, offer the option of locking their hands in their pockets instead of performing a hug.

"1-2-3 relax and b-r-e-a-t-h-e": Slow, deep breathing takes practice. Encourage a big breath in—through the nose—by saying, "Pretend you are smelling a beautiful flower or a batch of freshly baked cookies." For breathing out—through the mouth—lengthen the word "b-r-e-a-t-h-e" when you say it to signal that exhalation should be slow and gradual. Ask your child to imagine slowly blowing out candles on a birthday cake. Pretend your child's fingers are candles. Allow your child to feel the breath slowly tickling his or her fingers as the imaginary candles are blown out. See how long your child can feel the breath escaping.

"1-2-3 a calmer me": With the fourth line in the mantra, the hug is released and hands and arms are now relaxed at your child's side—or out of the pockets if your child has chosen this option. Lengthen the word "s-l-i-d-e" as hands and arms turn into jelly, causing the tight hug to loosen gradually. Say, "Pretend that your w-h-o-l-e body is made of jelly, from the top of your head to the tips of your toes." An easy way for your child to know the body is relaxing is to feel the shoulders dropping after the tight hug. Hopefully, in this more relaxed state, any urge to hit or kick will pass. Don't rush this step. An angry or frustrated brain needs time to stop and reset, making a calm and more comforting response possible. If your child is feeling big emotions in a frustrating moment, then the mantra may need to be repeated several times before the hug is finally unlocked.

Working Through the Book

As you read this book, have a discussion with your child. Talk about times when your emotions started spinning out of control and how you reacted. What would you do differently now? Think of situations when your child became angry and lashed out. What was the outcome? Children look to grown-ups to show and explain how to deal with feelings and disappointments. Adults who talk about emotions—and who provide positive and effective ways of coping with anger and frustration—help stop impulsive reactions from spinning into harmful and disruptive behaviors. Children also need tools to react effectively on their own, when adults are not present.

Begin to rehearse the mantra at times when your child is calm—for example, at the beginning of the day or as part of the bedtime routine. As the mantra is memorized, use it daily as unpredictable events happen. Recite the mantra with your child when you become frustrated as well. You may also start saying it, as a cue, when you see your child moving towards a situation known to be challenging, like when a younger sibling is about to grab a toy or when it's time to stop a favorite activity. The goal is to make the mantra automatic in times of distress. The more your child uses it—and sees it in action—the more automatic it should become. This practice, along with a reminder to "say the rhyme and do the actions if you get frustrated today," should help children stop and think before big reactions happen.

After Using the Mantra

What happens after using the mantra, in an upsetting situation, when your child is "a calmer me"? Talk to your child about what happened. Do not assume you know. Try to understand the event from your child's perspective. Ask what caused the frustration or anger. Give your child time to explain, without reacting or judging. Again, remind children that uncomfortable feelings are okay in frustrating situations and that *everyone* feels mad and upset sometimes. But children also need to know that choices can be made about *reacting* to those feelings. For example, if someone takes a toy, your child—after self-calming with the mantra—could ask for it back politely or suggest ways of playing with the toy cooperatively. If unhappy feelings persist, your child could seek help from an adult to solve the problem.

Sometimes big emotions and reactions keep happening even when you have tried many strategies. If upset feelings are overwhelming, making it very challenging for your child to learn at school, play at home, or get along with others, it may be helpful to consult a licensed psychologist or other mental health professional.

About the Authors

COLLEEN A. PATTERSON, MA, is a psychologist who has worked with children of all ages in hospital and school settings. She credits her parents with teaching her the importance of staying calm through challenges and adventures. A lifelong learner, she is always looking for new ways to keep balanced. *1-2-3 A Calmer Me* is her second book. Her award-winning first book, *How I Learn: A Kid's Guide to Learning Disability*, was published by Magination Press in 2014.

BRENDA S. MILES, PhD, is a pediatric neuropsychologist who has worked in hospital, rehabilitation, and school settings. She stays calm by spending time with her mom and dad, reading and writing books, watching movies, and playing with friends. She is the author of three other books for children, *Imagine a Rainbow: A Child's Guide for Soothing Pain*, *How I Learn: A Kid's Guide to Learning Disability*, and *Stickley Sticks to It!: A Frog's Guide to Getting Things Done*, all published by Magination Press.

About the Illustrator

CLAIRE KEAY lives in the south of England where she works from her small studio at home illustrating children's books and greeting cards as well as designing her own range of digital craft products.

About Magination Press

MAGINATION PRESS is an imprint of the American Psychological Association, the largest scientific and professional organization representing psychologists in the United States and the largest association of psychologists worldwide.